Text and Illustrations Copyright © 2015 by Schertevear Q. Watkins and Essence Watkins. Address all inquiries to:
Baobab Books
Email: bbfbooks@gmail.com

ISBN-13:
978-0692632529 (Baobab Publishing)

ISBN-10:
0692632522

Characters Like Me

Characters Like Me is a series that celebrates diversity by showcasing main characters from different backgrounds and with unique qualities. While drawing on cultural backgrounds, these stories are relatable to all children.

The purpose of Characters Like Me is not to limit children to reading stories, only about characters that share their own characteristics. These books help children celebrate their individuality and value the differences in others. As a result, all the stories are based on topics that interest every child and family.

Characters Like Me
on
and baobabpublishing.com

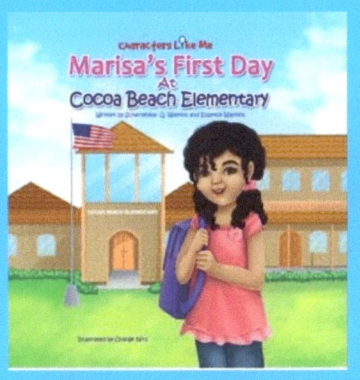

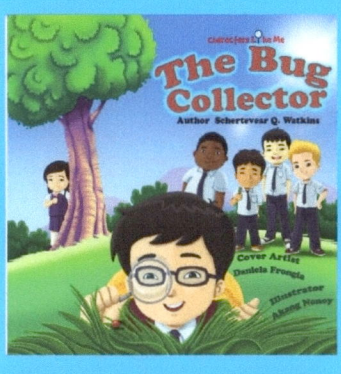

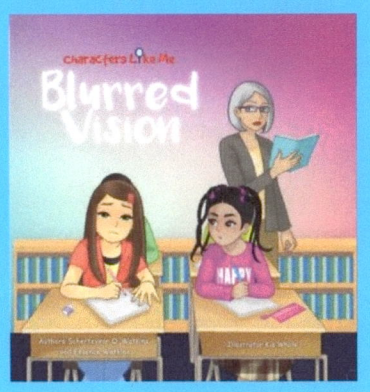

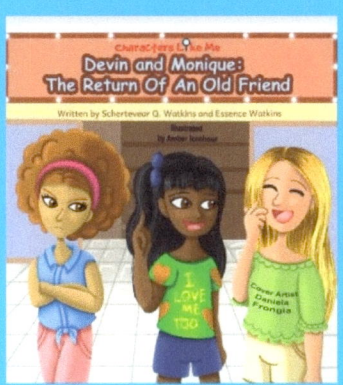

This Book Belongs To

_____

Mateo had been excited all week. He'd planned on going to the carnival with his mejores amigos (best buddies), Ian and Rodrigo when the weekend came. But with the weekend came heavy rain, and that meant no carnival.

Mateo was very upset that he couldn't go to the carnival. He was so aggravated and disappointed by the circumstances that he didn't know what to do with himself. Mateo asked his mom what he could do to keep his mind off the carnival and being bored.

"How about reading a book," Mateo's mom suggested.

So Mateo went into the house and up to his room. He took his mom's advice and read two books. In about fifteen minutes Mateo was bored again and calling his mom, "Mami I'm bored again." As he tossed the books onto his bedroom floor.

Mami came to Mateo's room. "Calmarse Hijo!" she ordered, asking Mateo to quiet down a bit. "Why don't you play with one of your new puzzles that Papa` bought you," Mateo's mom recommended.

Mateo put three puzzles together before calling his mom again. "Mami! Mami!" With a sigh, he pushed the puzzles aside, and the pieces scattered across the floor.

"Yes Mateo," Mateo's mom replied, "What is it now?"

"I'm bored again Mami," Mateo informed his mom. "I'm tired of putting puzzles together. Now what shall I do?"

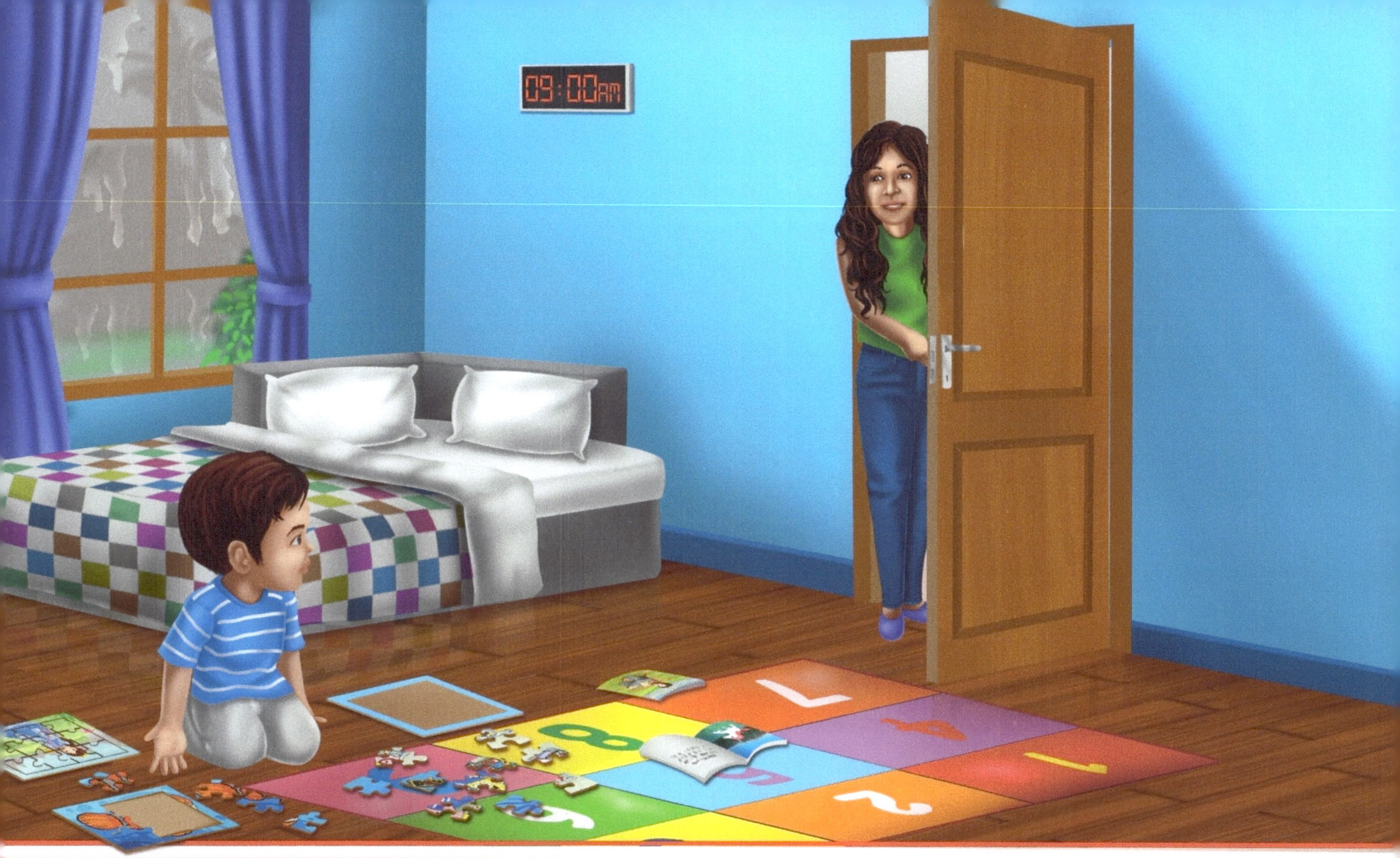
09:00AM

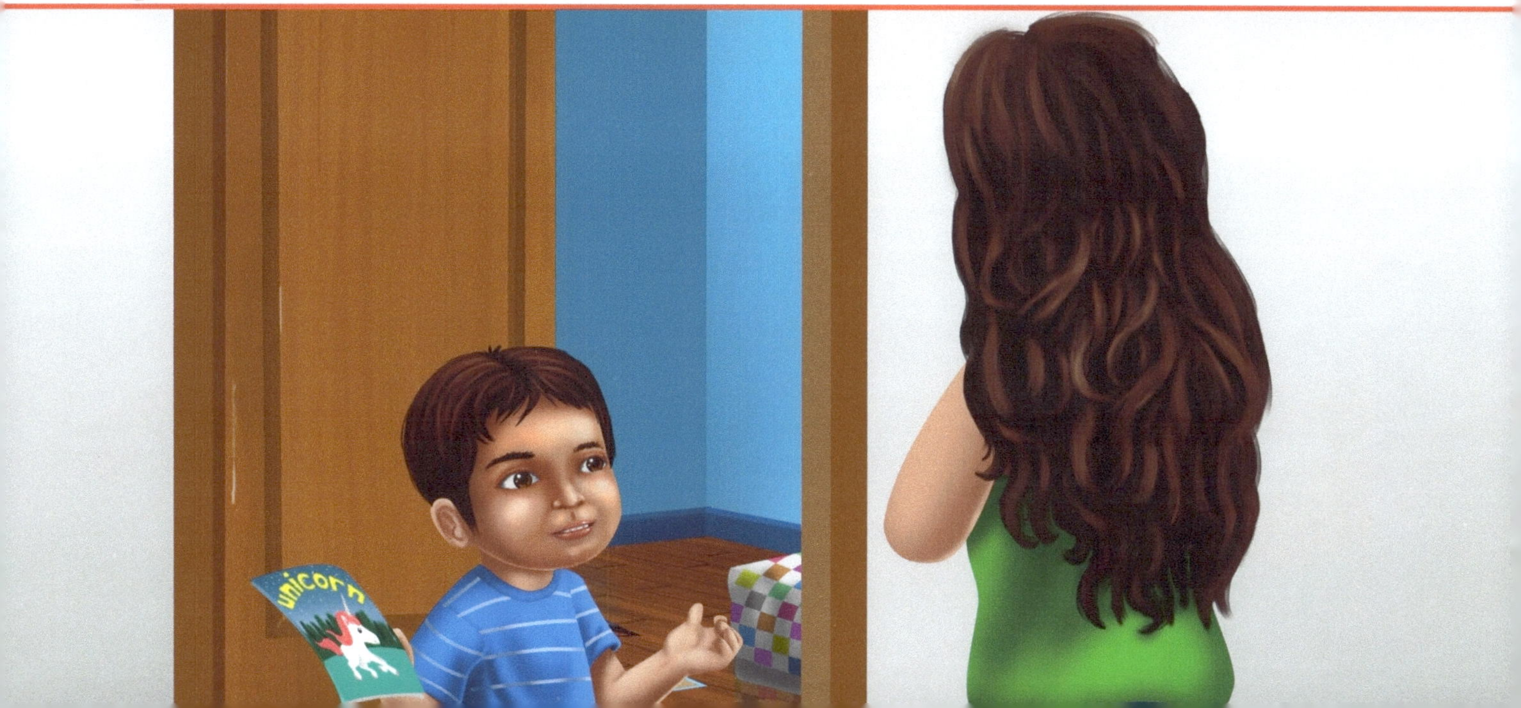
unicorn

Mateo's mom suggested this time that Mateo play some of his video games. Mami didn't really care for video games. But she really had a lot of house work to get done and she wasn't making much progress with Mateo calling her every other minute. Mateo agreed that games were a good idea. So Mami went back to her chores.

Mateo played four video games, and then he called his mom. "Mami, I have nothing to do!" Mateo left the video games and their cases laying on his bedroom floor.

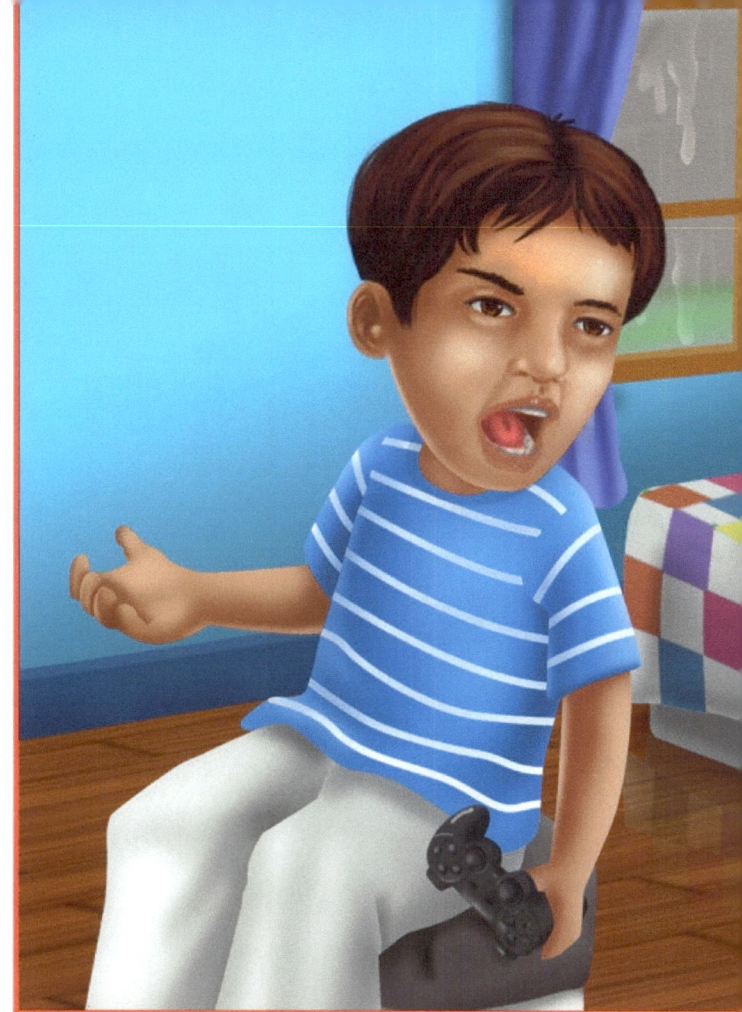

Mami came up and said, "Mateo, play with some of your toys."

Mateo thought that this was a great idea to keep him occupied. So, he played with action men, dinosaurs, cars, stuffed animals and blocks. An hour and twenty-seven minutes went by. This was the longest that Mateo had stayed entertained all morning. But like they say, "Nothing lasts forever."

When Mateo was done, he was done. His toys lay forgotten in every direction across his bedroom floor.
"Mami! I'm boooored!" Mateo called out as loud as he could.

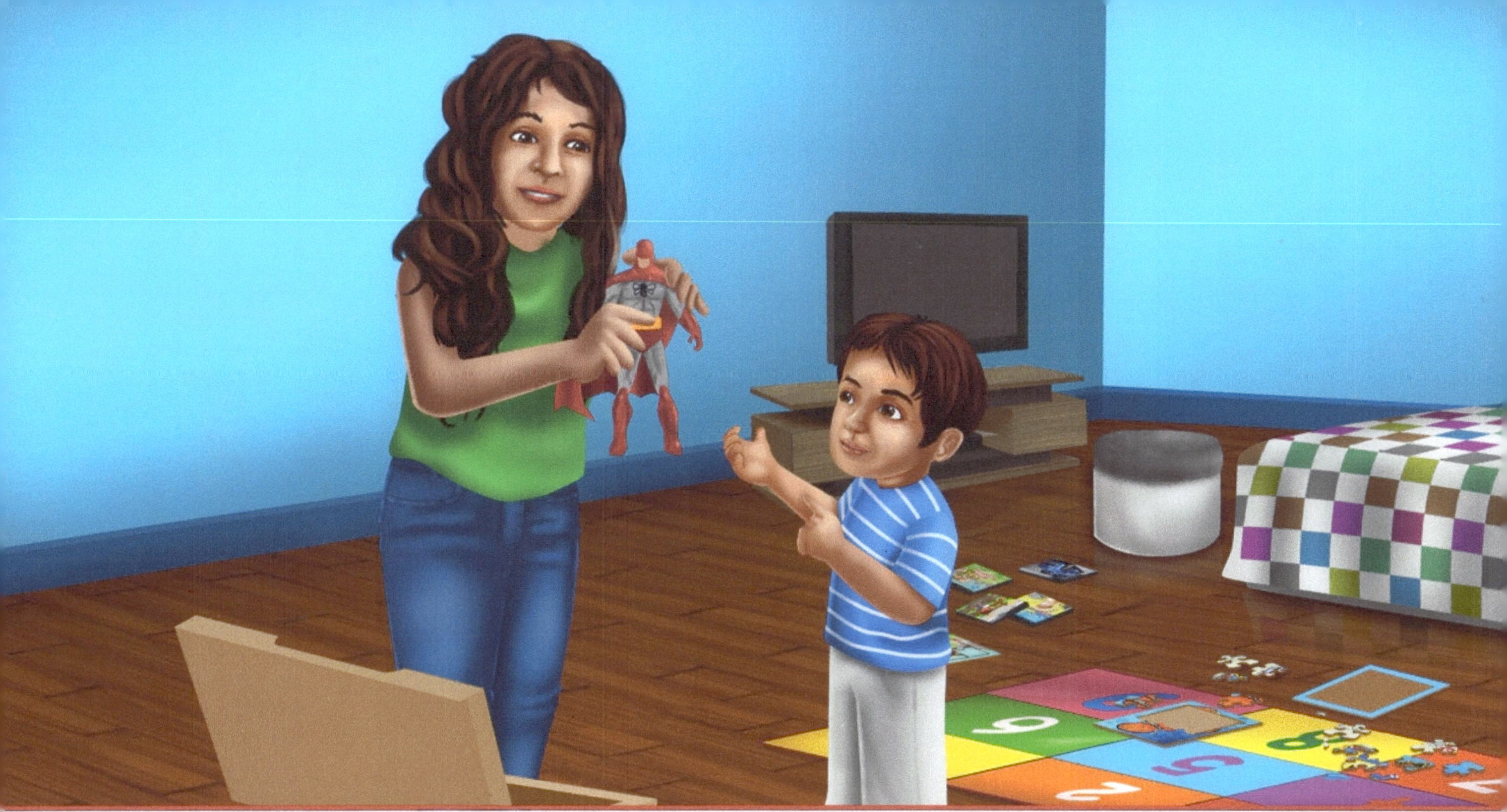

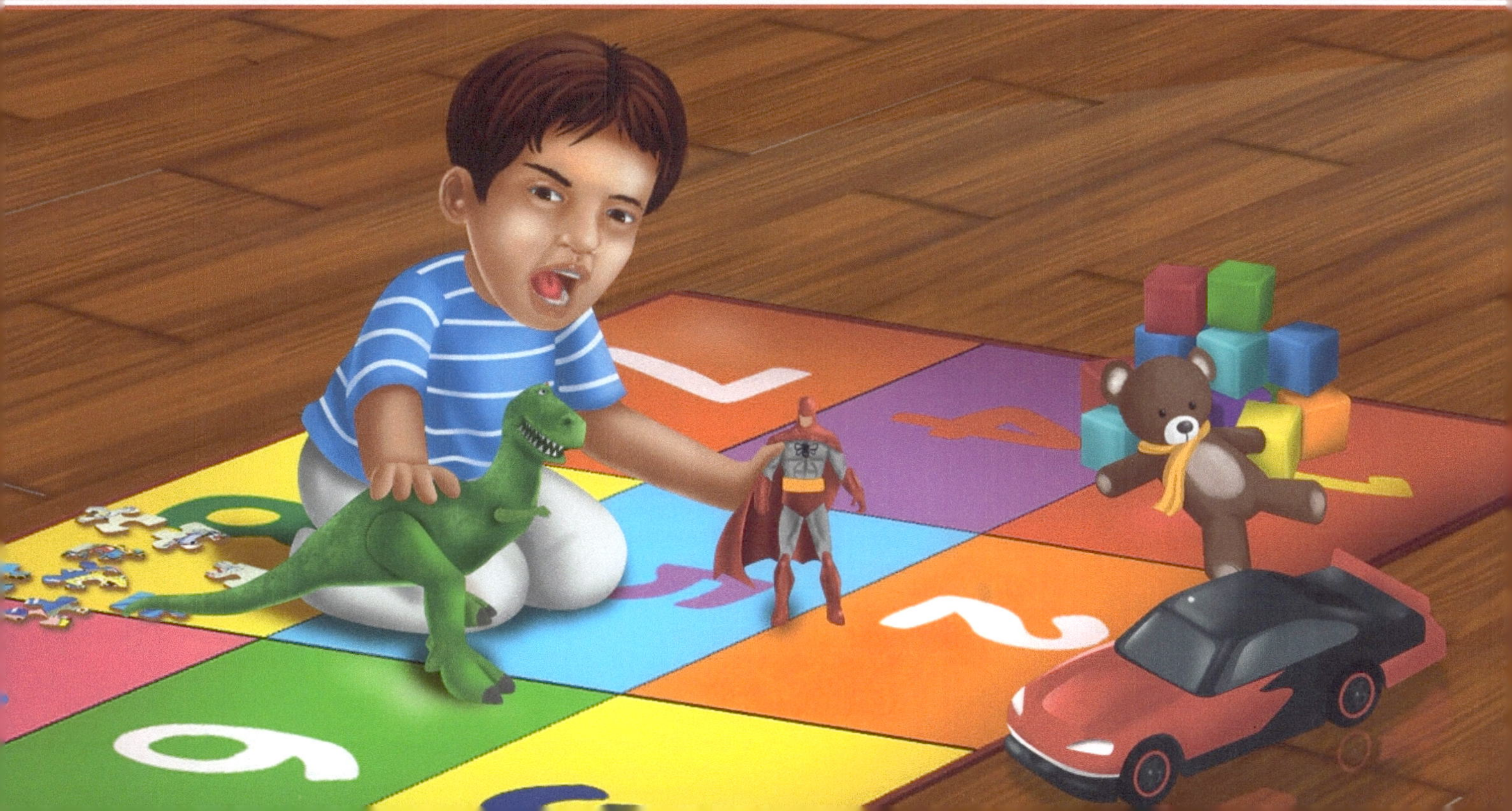

This time, when Mateo's mom came into his room, it was not just a mess, it was a complete disaster! This time Mateo's mom didn't suggest anything.

"You better clean up this mess!" Mami demanded. "Rapido!"

Mateo knew that his mom was not happy and that if he didn't clean the mess quickly, like she said, that he would be in big trouble. So, he cleaned the mess as quickly as he could. Then Mateo was bored once again.

Soon after Mateo was done cleaning his room, Mami called him down to eat lunch. She had ordered pizza and the delivery man came while Mateo was tidying up.

Mateo was happy while he was eating. He wasn't bored and didn't complain. But he did ask for more and more until his mom said, "No more, Mateo."

After lunch, Mateo decided to go into the living room. He sat on the sofa and watched cartoons for a while. He watched one space cartoon, one ninja cartoon, and a cartoon about pirates. After an hour of watching cartoons, Mateo was bored again. So, he decided to go back upstairs to his room.

On the way upstairs, Mateo passed by the large window in the foyer. He went over to the window to see if the rain had gone away. Disappointingly, it hadn't. But it had slowed down quite a bit. He still couldn't go to the carnival with Ian and Rodrigo though.

Mateo started feeling upset and aggravated again. He didn't want to stay downstairs with the big window where he could see all the rain coming down.

Mateo went back up to his room. When he got there, he remembered how he had already gotten bored doing everything that his mom suggested that he do in his room.

So he didn't ask his mom to help him this time. This time he thought of something to do on his own. He started jumping on his bed. He liked jumping on his bed. Mateo jumped higher and higher and higher, trying to find some fun in today.

"Are you jumping on that bed?" Mateo's mom asked, hearing his 'Yay!' and the bed squeaking and bumping up against the wall all the way downstairs.

"No Mami," Mateo fibbed.

"Jump on the bed, fall and bump that head," Mami warned.

But Mateo didn't listen to his mom's warning. He just continued jumping and jumping and screaming "Yay!" in delight.

Then it happened, Mateo fell off the bed onto the hard wood of his bedroom floor. He bruised his arm and he began to cry. Mami heard the boom from his fall and ran upstairs to Mateo's room and yelled, "What did I say about jumping on that bed!" Mateo's mom checked his boo-boo and suggested that he draw.

"What should I draw, Mami?" Mateo asked. "Un dia feliz." Mami suggested.

When Mateo's mom left to go back downstairs, Mateo looked in his nightstand drawer for paper and crayons to draw his Happy Day picture as his mom suggested. He found his crayons, but he didn't see his drawing tablet. So, Mateo had an idea. "I'll draw my "Happy Day" on my wall. Every day I awake and see it, I'll be happy!" Mateo thought.

But then Mateo hesitated, wondering if his mom would approve. "Ian has art painted on his wall," Mateo reasoned. "An artist came to his house and painted a whole town on his wall." So, Mateo figured that if it was okay for Ian to have his wall covered with art, then it should be okay for him too.

When Mateo was done with his "Happy Day" picture, he called his mom to come look.

"Wash this wall now!" Mateo's mom demanded. "Then you're going outside to play."

"But it's raining," Mateo replied.

"It's not coming down hard anymore. Just make sure you have your raincoat, rain hat, and rubber boots when you go out."

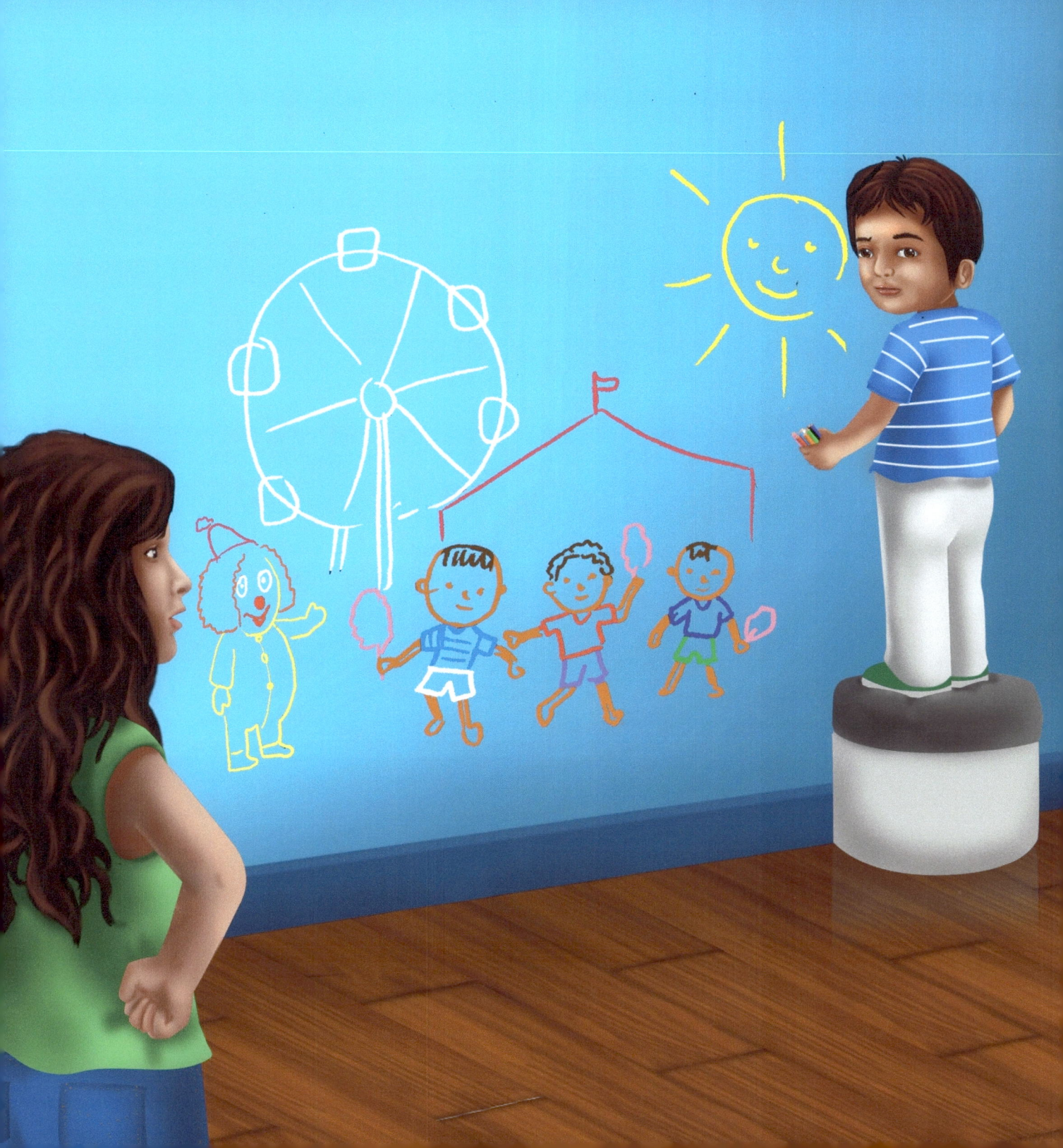

So, Mateo's mom gave him a pail of soapy water and a cloth. Mateo washed his wall until the crayon was unseen. Then he put on his raincoat, rain hat, and rubber boots to go outside.

When Mateo told his mom that he was ready to go out, she kissed his cheek and handed him an umbrella. "Stay in our yard," Mami instructed. Then she sent him on his way.

At first Mateo didn't know what to do outside in the rain. He'd never played in the rain before. After being outside for a few minutes watching the rain fall from the sky and trickle down his face, Mateo discovered that he liked being wet. Then Mateo held out his hands and opened his mouth to catch the rain. He stomped in puddles, danced and sang. "It's raining, it's pouring ..." Mateo sang as he skipped along the wet grass.

Mateo decided to throw rocks in
puddles to make a splash. Then he ran
swiftly through the wet grass. It was
fun playing in the rain. It was more fun
than he'd had all day.

Before Mateo knew it, the rain was gone. He heard the
neighbor across the street tell her little girl that there
would be clear skies tomorrow. So that meant that he
could go to the carnival this weekend with his mejores
amigos (best buddies), Ian and Rodrigo after all.

Thinking Questions

1. Why would the rain keep Mateo and his friends from going to the carnival playdate?
2. How do you think Mateo feels about his playdate being canceled?
3. How many shows does Mateo watch when he is downstairs in the living room?
4. Why is Mami upset with Mateo when she sees his "Happy Day" picture?
5. What is it that Mateo continues to forget to do when he's done playing with a toy?
6. Why do you suppose that Mami sent Mateo outside to play in the rain?

Recalling The Events

1. Why does Mateo seem sad at the beginning of the story as he and Mami stand in the doorway and look outside?
2. Where did Mateo want to go in this story?
3. Why did Mateo decide to jump on his bed instead of asking Mami to suggest something to keep him busy?
4. How does Mateo feel about playing in the rain?

More About The Story

1. What is the name of this book?
2. Who are the Authors of this book?
3. Who are the main characters in this story?
4. What is the mood of the main character? Why does he/she feel this way?
5. Does the main character resolve his/ her problem in the end? If so, how is the problem resolved?
6. Where does this story take place?
7. What is your opinion about the main character's problem and how it was solved?

FOLLOW THE AUTHOR.

Don't forget to REVIEW